This Topsy and Tim book belongs to

_____

Published by Ladybird Books Ltd
80 Strand London WC2R ORL
A Penguin Company

1 3 5 7 9 10 8 6 4 2

Red Boots
Yellow Boots

Jean and **Gareth Adamson**

When Topsy and Tim looked out of
the window for the first time on
Monday morning the rain was
pouring down.

Mr Fen, who lived next door, was holding a big, stripey umbrella.

"Nice weather – for ducks!" he called.

Two pairs of boots were standing in the hall—yellow boots for Topsy and red boots for Tim.

"I'm not wearing *my* boots," said Tim.

Mummy pulled and Topsy pushed –
and Topsy had her boots on, ready
to go to playgroup.
"Now you, Tim," said Mummy.

Tim was very naughty and stamped
and shouted, *"I don't want my boots."*
"All right," said Mummy. "You can
wear your ordinary shoes. It's time you
learned a lesson."

So when Tim and Topsy set off for playgroup, Topsy was wearing her big yellow boots but Tim was wearing his ordinary shoes.

Tim could run faster in his ordinary shoes, so he danced in circles round Topsy shouting, "Funny boots! Funny boots!"

Tim walked backwards in front of
Topsy and put out his tongue.
And then he stepped right into a
deep, deep, puddle.

"Yow!" he howled. "My feet are all cold and wet."

Topsy walked right through the big puddle and didn't get cold or wet at all.

"Come inside quickly, children,"
called Miss Maypole, "and change
into your dry shoes."

"Why ever aren't you wearing your big red boots, Tim?" asked Miss Maypole. "He wouldn't put them on," laughed Topsy.

"What a silly little boy!" said Miss Maypole. "I shall have to hang your wet socks up to dry."

Tim had to sit on a table with his bare feet dangling.

When Mummy came to fetch them home she had Tim's big red boots in her zip-up bag.

He put them on quickly.

Topsy and Tim plodged through all
the big puddles on the way home.
"Good old red boots!" said Tim.

Talk about the story.

Tim's boots are red.
Topsy's boots are yellow.
Can you match the pairs here?

Topsy and Tim planted some seeds.
Talk about what happened after that.

Topsy and Tim are looking for the
missing words in these rhymes
about the rain.
Can you say the words?

Rain, 🌧, go away
Come again another day.

Incy Wincy 🕷
Climbed up the spout.
Down came a rain storm,
And washed the 🕷 out.
When the ☀ came out again,
And dried up all the 🌧
Incy Wincy Spider climbed the spout again.

Help Topsy and Tim to work out
the puzzles.

Which is wet?
Which is dry?

Which is up?
Which is down?

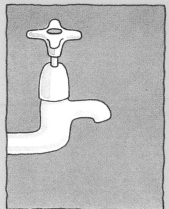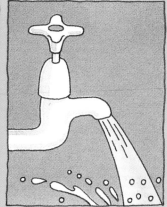

Which is on?
Which is off?

Which is high?
Which is low?